UNDER
THE
JAGUAR
SUN

BY ITALO CALVINO AND AVAILABLE FROM
HARCOURT BRACE JOVANOVICH, PUBLISHERS
IN HARVEST/HBJ PAPERBACK EDITIONS

The Baron in the Trees
The Castle of Crossed Destinies
Cosmicomics
Difficult Loves
If on a winter's night a traveler
Invisible Cities
Marcovaldo, or
The seasons in the city
Mr. Palomar
The Nonexistent Knight *and*
The Cloven Viscount
t zero
Under the Jaguar Sun
The Uses of Literature
The Watcher and Other Stories

AVAILABLE FROM
HARCOURT BRACE JOVANOVICH, PUBLISHERS,
IN A HARDCOVER EDITION ONLY
Italian Folktales

PUBLISHED BY HARVARD UNIVERSITY PRESS
Six Memos for the Next Millennium

ITALO
CALVINO

UNDER
THE
JAGUAR
SUN

Translated by William Weaver

A Harvest/HBJ Book
A Helen and Kurt Wolff Book
Harcourt Brace Jovanovich, Publishers
SAN DIEGO   NEW YORK   LONDON

HBJ

Copyright © 1986 by Garzanti Editore
English translation copyright © 1988 by
Harcourt Brace Jovanovich, Inc.

"Under the Jaguar Sun" was first published as "The Jaguar Sun"
in *The New Yorker*, English translation copyright © 1983
by Harcourt Brace Jovanovich, Inc.
"The Name, the Nose" was first published in *Antaeus*,
English translation copyright © 1976 by Harcourt Brace Jovanovich, Inc.
Both stories originally appeared in slightly different form.

Requests for permission to make copies of any
part of the work should be mailed to:
Permissions Department,
Harcourt Brace Jovanovich, Publishers,
Orlando, Florida 32887.

Library of Congress Cataloging-in-Publication Data

Calvino, Italo.
[Short stories. English. Selections]
Under the jaguar sun / Calvino Italo; translated by William Weaver.
p.   cm.
Translated from the Italian.
"A Helen and Kurt Wolff Book."
Contents: Under the jaguar sun—A king listens—The name, the nose.
ISBN 0-15-192820-7
ISBN 0-15-692794-2 (Harvest/HBJ: pbk.)
1. Calvino, Italo—Translations, English.   I. Title.
PQ4809.A45A6   1988
853'.914—dc19   88-835

Designed by Michael Farmer
Printed in the United States of America
First Harvest/HBJ edition 1990
A B C D E

Contents

UNDER
THE
JAGUAR
SUN

"OAXACA" is pronounced "Wa*haka*." Originally, the hotel where we were staying had been the Convent of Santa Catalina. The first thing we noticed was a painting in a little room leading to the bar. The bar was called Las Novicias. The painting was a large, dark canvas that portrayed a young nun and an old priest standing side by side; their hands, slightly apart from their sides, almost touched. The figures were rather stiff for an eighteenth-century picture; the painting had the somewhat crude grace characteristic of colonial art, but it conveyed a distressing sensation, like an ache of contained suffering.

The lower part of the painting was filled by a long caption, written in cramped lines in an angular, italic hand, white on black. The words devoutly celebrated the life and death of the two characters, who had been chaplain and abbess of the convent (she, of noble birth, had entered it as a novice at the age of eighteen). The reason for their being painted together was the extraordinary love (this word, in the pious Spanish prose, appeared charged with ultra-terrestrial yearning) that had bound the abbess and her confessor for thirty years, a love so great (the word in its spiritual sense sublimated but did not erase the physical emotion) that when the priest came to die, the abbess, twenty years younger, in the space of a single day fell ill and literally expired of love (the word blazed with a truth in which all meanings converge), to join him in Heaven.

Olivia, whose Spanish is better than mine, helped me decipher the story, suggesting to me the translation of some obscure expressions, and these words proved to be the only ones we exchanged during and after the reading, as if we had found ourselves in the presence of a drama, or of a happiness, that made any comment out of place. Something intimidated us—or, rather, frightened us, or, more precisely, filled us with a kind of uneasiness. So I will try to describe what I felt: the sense of a lack, a consuming void. What Olivia was thinking, since she remained silent, I cannot guess.

Then Olivia spoke. She said, "I would like to eat *chiles en nogada.*" And, walking like somnambulists, not quite sure we were touching the ground, we headed for the dining room.

In the best moments of a couple's life, it happens: I immediately reconstructed the train of Olivia's thought, with no need of further speech, because the same sequence of associations had unrolled in my mind, though

in a more foggy, murky way. Without her, I would
never have gained awareness of it.

Our trip through Mexico had already lasted over a
week. A few days earlier, in Tepotzotlán, in a restaurant whose tables were set among the orange trees of
another convent's cloister, we had savored dishes pre-
pared (at least, so we were told) according to the tra-
ditional recipes of the nuns. We had eaten a *tamal de
elote*—a fine semolina of sweet corn, that is, with ground
pork and very hot pepper, all steamed in a bit of corn-
husk—and then *chiles en nogada*, which were reddish
brown, somewhat wrinkled little peppers, swimming in
a walnut sauce whose harshness and bitter aftertaste were
drowned in a creamy, sweetish surrender.

After that, for us, the thought of nuns called up the
flavors of an elaborate and bold cuisine, bent on making the flavors' highest notes vibrate, juxtaposing them
in modulations, in chords, and especially in dissonances
that would assert themselves as an incomparable experience—a point of no return, an absolute possession
exercised on the receptivity of all the senses.

The Mexican friend who had accompanied us on that
excursion, Salustiano Velazco by name, in answering
Olivia's inquiries about these recipes of conventual gas-
tronomy, lowered his voice as if confiding indelicate
secrets to us. It was his way of speaking—or, rather,
one of his ways; the copious information Salustiano
supplied (about the history and customs and nature of
his country his erudition was inexhaustible) was either
stated emphatically like a war proclamation or slyly in-

sinuated as if it were charged with all sorts of implied meanings.

Olivia remarked that such dishes involved hours and hours of work and, even before that, a long series of experiments and adjustments. "Did these nuns spend their whole day in the kitchen?" she asked, imagining entire lives devoted to the search for new blends of ingredients, new variations in the measurements, to alert and patient mixing, to the handing down of an intricate, precise lore.

"*Tenían sus criadas*," Salustiano answered. ("They had their servants.") And he explained to us that when the daughters of noble families entered the convent, they brought their maids with them; thus, to satisfy the venial whims of gluttony, the only cravings allowed them, the nuns could rely on a swarm of eager, tireless helpers. And as far as they themselves were concerned, they had only to conceive and compare and correct the recipes that expressed their fantasies confined within those walls: the fantasies, after all, of sophisticated women, bright and introverted and complex women who needed absolutes, whose reading told of ecstasies and transfigurations, martyrs and tortures, women with conflicting calls in their blood, genealogies in which the descendants of the conquistadores mingled with those of Indian princesses or slaves, women with childhood recollections of the fruits and fragrances of a succulent vegetation, thick with ferments, though growing from those sun-baked plateaus.

Nor should sacred architecture be overlooked, the

background to the lives of those religious; it, too, was impelled by the same drive toward the extreme that led to the exacerbation of flavors amplified by the blaze of the most spicy *chiles*. Just as colonial baroque set no limits on the profusion of ornament and display, in which God's presence was identified in a closely calculated delirium of brimming, excessive sensations, so the curing of the hundred or more native varieties of hot peppers carefully selected for each dish opened vistas of a flaming ecstasy.

At Tepotzotlán, we visited the church the Jesuits had built in the eighteenth century for their seminary (and no sooner was it consecrated than they had to abandon it, as they were expelled from Mexico forever): a theater-church, all gold and bright colors, in a dancing and acrobatic baroque, crammed with swirling angels, garlands, panoplies of flowers, shells. Surely the Jesuits meant to compete with the splendor of the Aztecs, whose ruined temples and palaces—the royal palace of Quetzalcóatl!—still stood, to recall a rule imposed through the impressive effects of a grandiose, transfiguring art. There was a challenge in the air, in this dry and thin air at an altitude of two thousand meters: the ancient rivalry between the civilizations of America and Spain in the art of bewitching the senses with dazzling seductions. And from architecture this rivalry extended to cuisine, where the two civilizations had merged, or perhaps where the conquered had triumphed, strong in the condiments born from their very soil. Through the white hands of novices and the brown hands of lay sisters, the cuisine of the new Indo-Hispanic civilization had become also the field of battle between the aggressive ferocity of the ancient gods of the mesa and the sinuous excess of the baroque religion.

On the supper menu we didn't find *chiles en nogada*. From one locality to the next the gastronomic lexicon varied, always offering new terms to be recorded and new sensations to be defined. Instead, we found *guacamole*, to be scooped up with crisp tortillas that snap into many shards and dip like spoons into the thick cream (the fat softness of the *aguacate*—the Mexican national fruit, known to the rest of the world under the distorted name of "avocado"—is accompanied and underlined by the angular dryness of the tortilla, which, for its part, can have many flavors, pretending to have none); then *guajolote con mole poblano*—that is, turkey with Puebla-style *mole* sauce, one of the noblest among the many *moles*, and most laborious (the preparation never takes less than two days), and most complicated, because it requires several different varieties of *chile*, as well as garlic, onion, cinnamon, cloves, pepper, cumin, coriander, and sesame, almonds, raisins, and peanuts, with a touch of chocolate; and finally *quesadillas* (another kind of tortilla, really, for which cheese is incorporated in the dough, garnished with ground meat and refried beans).

Right in the midst of chewing, Olivia's lips paused, almost stopped, though without completely interrupting their continuity of movement, which slowed down, as if reluctant to allow an inner echo to fade, while her gaze became fixed, intent on no specific object, in apparent alarm. Her face had a special concentration that I had observed during meals ever since we began our trip to Mexico. I followed the tension as it moved from her lips to her nostrils, flaring one moment, contracting the next, (the plasticity of the nose is quite limited—especially for a delicate, harmonious nose like Olivia's—and each barely perceptible attempt to expand the capacity of the nostrils in the longitudinal direction actually makes them thinner, while the corresponding reflex movement, accentuating their breadth, then seems a kind of withdrawal of the whole nose into the surface of the face).

What I have just said might suggest that, in eating, Olivia became closed into herself, absorbed with the inner course of her sensations; in reality, on the contrary, the desire her whole person expressed was that of communicating to me what she was tasting: communicating with me through flavors, or communicating with flavors through a double set of taste buds, hers and mine. "Did you taste that? Are you tasting it?" she was asking me, with a kind of anxiety, as if at that same moment our incisors had pierced an identically composed morsel and the same drop of savor had been caught by the membranes of my tongue and of hers. "Is it *cilantro*? Can't you taste *cilantro*?" she insisted, referring to an herb whose local name hadn't allowed us to identify it with certainty (was it coriander, perhaps?) and of which a little thread in the morsel we were chewing sufficed to transmit to the nostrils a sweetly pungent emotion, like an impalpable intoxication.

Olivia's need to involve me in her emotions pleased

me greatly, because it showed that I was indispensable
to her and that, for her, the pleasures of existence could
be appreciated only if we shared them. Our subjective,
individual selves, I was thinking, find their amplifica-
tion and completion only in the unity of the couple. I
needed confirmation of this conviction all the more since,
from the beginning of our Mexican journey, the physical bond between Olivia and me was going through a
phase of rarefaction, if not eclipse: a momentary phe-
nomenon, surely, and not in itself disturbing—part of
the normal ups and downs to which, over a long period, the life of every couple is subject. And I couldn't
help remarking how certain manifestations of Olivia's
vital energy, certain prompt reactions or delays on her
part, yearnings or throbs, continued to take place before my eyes, losing none of their intensity, with only
one significant difference: their stage was no longer the
bed of our embraces but a dinner table.

During the first few days I expected the gradual kin-
dling of the palate to spread quickly to all our senses. I
was mistaken: aphrodisiac this cuisine surely was, but
in itself and for itself (this is what I thought to understand, and what I am saying applies only to us at that
moment; I cannot speak for others or for us if we had
been in a different humor). It stimulated desires, in other
words, that sought their satisfaction only within the very
sphere of sensation that had aroused them—in eating
new dishes, therefore, that would generate and extend
those same desires. We were thus in the ideal situation
for imagining what the love between the abbess and the

chaplain might have been like: a love that, in the eyes of the world and in their own eyes, could have been perfectly chaste and at the same time infinitely carnal in that experience of flavors gained through secret and subtle complicity.

"Complicity": the word, the moment it came into my mind—referring not only to the nun and the priest but also to Olivia and me—heartened me. Because if what Olivia sought was complicity in the almost obsessive passion that had seized her, then this suggested we were not losing—as I had feared—a parity between us. In fact, it had seemed to me during the last few days that Olivia, in her gustatory exploration, had wanted to keep me in a subordinate position: a presence necessary, indeed, but subaltern, obliging me to observe the relationship between her and food as a confidant or as a compliant pander. I dispelled this irksome notion that had somehow or other occurred to me. In reality, our complicity could not be more total, precisely because we experienced the same passion in different ways, in accord with our temperaments: Olivia more sensitive to perceptive nuances and endowed with a more analytical memory, where every recollection remained distinct and unmistakable, I tending more to define experiences verbally and conceptually, to mark the ideal line of journey within ourselves contemporaneously with our geographical journey. In fact, this was a conclusion of mine that Olivia had instantly adopted (or perhaps Olivia had been the one to prompt the idea and I had simply proposed it to her again in words of my own):

the true journey, as the introjection of an "outside" different from our normal one, implies a complete change of nutrition, a digesting of the visited country—its fauna and flora and its culture (not only the different culinary practices and condiments but the different implements used to grind the flour or stir the pot)—making it pass between the lips and down the esophagus. This is the only kind of travel that has a meaning nowadays, when everything visible you can see on television without rising from your easy chair. (And you mustn't rebut that the same result can be achieved by visiting the exotic restaurants of our big cities; they so counterfeit the reality of the cuisine they claim to follow that, as far as our deriving real knowledge is concerned, they are the equivalent not of an actual locality but of a scene reconstructed and shot in a studio.)

ALL the same, in the course of our trip Olivia and I saw everything there was to see (no small exploit, in quantity or quality). For the following morning we had planned a visit to the excavations at Monte Albán, and the guide came for us at the hotel promptly with a little bus. In the sunny, arid countryside grow the agaves used for mescal and tequila, and *nopales* (which we call prickly pears) and cereus—all thorns—and jacaranda, with its blue flowers. The road climbs up into the mountains. Monte Albán, among the heights surrounding a valley, is a complex of ruins: temples, reliefs, grand stairways, platforms for human sacrifice. Horror, sacredness, and mystery are consolidated by tourism, which dictates preordained forms of behavior, the modest surrogates of those rites. Contemplating these stairs, we try to imagine the hot blood spurting from the breast split by the stone axe of the priest.

Three civilizations succeeded one another at Monte Albán, each shifting the same blocks: the Zapotecs building over the works of the Olmecs, and the Mixtecs doing the same to those of the Zapotecs. The calendars of the ancient Mexican civilizations, carved on the reliefs, represent a cyclic, tragic concept of time: every fifty-two years the universe ended, the gods died, the temples were destroyed, every celestial and terrestrial thing changed its name. Perhaps the peoples that history defines as the successive occupants of these territories were merely a single people, whose continuity was never broken even through a series of massacres like those the reliefs depict. Here are the conquered villages, their names written in hieroglyphics, and the god of the village, his head hung upside down; here are the chained prisoners of war, the severed heads of the victims.

The guide to whom the travel agency entrusted us, a burly man named Alonso, with flattened features like an Olmec head (or Mixtec? Zapotec?), points out to us, with exuberant mime, the famous bas-reliefs called "Los Danzantes." Only some of the carved figures, he says, are portraits of dancers, with their legs in movement (Alonso performs a few steps); others might be astronomers, raising one hand to shield their eyes and study the stars (Alonso strikes an astronomer's pose). But for

the most part, he says, they represent women giving
birth (Alonso acts this out). We learn that this temple
was meant to ward off difficult childbirths; the reliefs
were perhaps votive images. Even the dance, for that
matter, served to make births easier, through magic mimesis—especially when the baby came out feet first
(Alonso performs the magic mimesis). One relief de-
picts a cesarean operation, complete with uterus and
Fallopian tubes (Alonso, more brutal than ever, mimes
the entire female anatomy, to demonstrate that a sole
surgical torment linked births and deaths).

Everything in our guide's gesticulation takes on a
truculent significance, as if the temples of the sacrifices
cast their shadow on every act and every thought. When
the most propitious date had been set, in accordance
with the stars, the sacrifices were accompanied by the
revelry of dances, and even births seemed to have no
purpose beyond supplying new soldiers for the wars to
capture victims. Though some figures are shown running or wrestling or playing football, according to
Alonso these are not peaceful athletic competitions but,
rather, the games of prisoners forced to compete in order to determine which of them would be the first to
ascend the altar.

"And the loser in the games was chosen for the sacrifice?" I ask.

"No! The winner!" Alonso's face becomes radiant.
"To have your chest split open by the obsidian knife
was an honor!" And in a crescendo of ancestral patri-
otism, just as he had boasted of the excellence of the

scientific knowledge of the ancient peoples, so now this worthy descendant of the Olmeçs feels called upon to exalt the offering of a throbbing human heart to the sun to assure that the dawn would return each morning and illuminate the world.

That was when Olivia asked, "But what did they do with the victims' bodies afterward?"

Alonso stopped.

"Those limbs—I mean, those entrails," Olivia insisted. "They were offered to the gods, I realize that. But, practically speaking, what happened to them? Were they burned?"

No, they weren't burned.

"Well, what then? Surely a gift to the gods couldn't be buried, left to rot in the ground."

"*Los zopilotes,*" Alonso said. "The vultures. They were the ones who cleared the altars and carried the offerings to Heaven."

The vultures. "Always?" Olivia asked further, with an insistence I could not explain to myself.

Alonso was evasive, tried to change the subject; he was in a hurry to show us the passages that connected the priests' houses with the temples, where they made their appearance, their faces covered by terrifying masks. Our guide's pedagogical enthusiasm had something irritating about it, because it gave the impression he was imparting to us a lesson that was simplified so that it would enter our poor profane heads, though he actually knew far more, things he kept to himself and took care not to tell us. Perhaps this was what Olivia had sensed and what, after a certain point, made her maintain a closed, vexed silence through the rest of our visit to the excavations and on the jolting bus that brought us back to Oaxaca.

Along the road, all curves, I tried to catch Olivia's eye as she sat facing me, but thanks to the bouncing of the bus or the difference in the level of our seats, I realized my gaze was resting not on her eyes but on her teeth (she kept her lips parted in a pensive expression), which I happened to be seeing for the first time not as the radiant glow of a smile but as the instruments most suited to their purpose: to be dug into flesh, to sever it, tear it. And as you try to read a person's thoughts in the expression of his eyes, so now I looked at those strong, sharp teeth and sensed there a restrained desire, an expectation.

As we reentered the hotel and headed for the large lobby (the former chapel of the convent), which we had to cross to reach the wing where our room was, we were struck by a sound like a cascade of water flowing and splashing and gurgling in a thousand rivulets and eddies and jets. The closer we got, the more this homogeneous noise was broken down into a complex of chirps, trills, caws, clucks, as of a flock of birds flapping their wings in an aviary. From the doorway (the room was a few steps lower than the corridor), we saw an expanse of little spring hats on the heads of ladies seated around tea tables. Throughout the country a campaign was in progress for the election of a new president of the republic, and the wife of the favored candidate was giving a tea party of impressive proportions for the wives of the prominent men of Oaxaca. Under the broad, empty vaulted ceiling, three hundred Mexican ladies were conversing all at once; the spectacular acoustical event that had immediately subdued us was produced by their voices mingled with the tinkling of cups and spoons and of knives cutting slices of cake. Looming over the assembly was a gigantic full-color picture of a round-faced lady with her black, smooth hair drawn straight back, wearing a blue dress of which only the buttoned collar could be seen; it was not unlike the official portraits of Chairman Mao Tse-tung, in other words.

To reach the patio and, from it, our stairs, we had to pick our way among the little tables of the reception. We were already close to the far exit when, from a table at the back of the hall, one of the few male guests rose and came toward us, arms extended. It was our friend Salustiano Velazco, a member of the would-be president's staff and, in that capacity, a participant in the more delicate stages of the electoral campaign. We hadn't seen him since leaving the capital, and to show us, with all his ebullience, his joy on seeing us again and to inquire about the latest stages of our journey (and perhaps to escape momentarily that atmosphere in which the triumphal female predominance compromised his chivalrous certitude of male supremacy) he left his place of honor at the symposium and accompanied us into the patio.

Instead of asking us about what we had seen, he be-

gan by pointing out the things we had surely failed to
see in the places we had visited and could have seen
only if he had been with us—a conversational formula
that impassioned connoisseurs of a country feel obliged
to adopt with visiting friends, always with the best intentions, though it successfully spoils the pleasure of
those who have returned from a trip and are quite proud
of their experiences, great or small. The convivial din
of the distinguished gynaeceum followed us even into
the patio and drowned at least half the words he and
we spoke, so I was never sure he wasn't reproaching us
for not having seen the very things we had just finished
telling him we had seen.

"And today we went to Monte Albán," I quickly
informed him, raising my voice. "The stairways, the
reliefs, the sacrificial altars . . ."

Salustiano put his hand to his mouth, then waved it
in midair—a gesture that, for him, meant an emotion
too great to be expressed in words. He began by fur-
nishing us archeological and ethnographical details I
would have very much liked to hear sentence by sentence, but they were lost in the reverberations of the
feast. From his gestures and the scattered words I managed to catch ("*Sangre . . . obsidiana . . . divinidad
solar*"), I realized he was talking about the human sacrifices and was speaking with a mixture of awed partic-
ipation and sacred horror—an attitude distinguished
from that of our crude guide by a greater awareness of
the cultural implications.

Quicker than I, Olivia managed to follow Salustiano's speech better, and now she spoke up, to ask him something. I realized she was repeating the question she had asked Alonso that afternoon: "What the vultures didn't carry off—what happened to that, afterward?"

Salustiano's eyes flashed knowing sparks at Olivia, and I also grasped then the purpose behind her question, especially as Salustiano assumed his confidential, abettor's tone. It seemed that, precisely because they were softer, his words now overcame more easily the barrier of sound that separated us.

"Who knows? The priests . . . This was also a part of the rite—I mean among the Aztecs, the people we know better. But even about them, not much is known. These were secret ceremonies. Yes, the ritual meal . . . The priest assumed the functions of the god, and so the victim, divine food . . ."

Was this Olivia's aim? To make him admit this? She insisted further, "But how did it take place? The meal . . ."

"As I say, there are only some suppositions. It seems that the princes, the warriors also joined in. The victim was already part of the god, transmitting divine strength." At this point, Salustiano changed his tone and became proud, dramatic, carried away. "Only the warrior who had captured the sacrificed prisoner could not touch his flesh. He remained apart, weeping."

Olivia still didn't seem satisfied. "But this flesh—in order to eat it . . . The way it was cooked, the sacred cuisine, the seasoning—is anything known about that?"

Salustiano became thoughtful. The banqueting ladies

had redoubled their noise, and now Salustiano seemed to become hypersensitive to their sounds; he tapped his ear with one finger, signalling that he couldn't go on in all that racket. "Yes, there must have been some rules. Of course, that food couldn't be consumed without a special ceremony . . . the due honor . . . the respect for the sacrificed, who were brave youths . . . respect for the gods . . . flesh that couldn't be eaten just for the sake of eating, like any ordinary food. And the flavor . . ."

"They say it isn't good to eat?"

"A strange flavor, they say."

"It must have required seasoning—strong stuff."

"Perhaps that flavor had to be hidden. All other flavors had to be brought together, to hide that flavor."

And Olivia asked, "But the priests . . . About the cooking of it—they didn't leave any instructions? Didn't hand down anything?"

Salustiano shook his head. "A mystery. Their life was shrouded in mystery."

And Olivia—Olivia now seemed to be prompting him. "Perhaps that flavor emerged, all the same—even through the other flavors."

Salustiano put his fingers to his lips, as if to filter what he was saying. "It was a sacred cuisine. It had to celebrate the harmony of the elements achieved through sacrifice—a terrible harmony, flaming, incandescent . . ." He fell suddenly silent, as if sensing he had gone too far, and as if the thought of the repast had called him to his duty, he hastily apologized for not being able to stay longer with us. He had to go back to his place at the table.

WAITING for evening to fall, we sat in one of the cafés under the arcades of the *zócalo*, the regular little square that is the heart of every old city of the colony—green, with short, carefully pruned trees called *almendros*, though they bear no resemblance to almond trees. The tiny paper flags and the banners that greeted the official candidate did their best to convey a festive air to the *zócalo*. The proper Oaxaca families strolled under the arcades. American hippies waited for the old woman who supplied them with *mescalina*. Ragged vendors unfurled colored fabrics on the ground. From another square nearby came the echo of the loudspeakers of a sparsely attended rally of the opposition. Crouched on the ground, heavy women were frying tortillas and greens.

In the kiosk in the middle of the square, an orchestra was playing, bringing back to me reassuring memories of evenings in a familiar, provincial Europe I was old enough to have known and forgotten. But the memory was like a trompe-l'oeil, and when I examined it a little, it gave me a sense of multiplied distance, in space and in time. Wearing black suits and neckties, the musicians, with their dark, impassive Indian faces, played for the varicolored, shirtsleeved tourists—inhabitants, it seemed, of a perpetual summer—for parties of old men and women, meretriciously young in all the gleam of their dentures, and for groups of the really young, hunched over and meditative, as if waiting for age to come and whiten their blond beards and flowing hair; bundled in rough clothes, weighed down by their knapsacks, they looked like the allegorical figures of winter in old calendars.

"Perhaps time has come to an end, the sun has grown weary of rising, Chronos dies of starvation for want of victims to devour, the ages and the seasons are turned upside down," I said.

"Perhaps the death of time concerns only us," Olivia answered. "We who tear one another apart, pretending not to know it, pretending not to taste flavors anymore."

"You mean that here—that they need stronger flavors here because they know, because here they ate . . ."

"The same as at home, even now. Only we no longer know it, no longer dare look, the way they did. For them there was no mystification: the horror was right there, in front of their eyes. They ate as long as there was a bone left to pick clean, and that's why the flavors . . ."

"To hide that flavor?" I said, again picking up Salustiano's chain of hypotheses.

"Perhaps it couldn't be hidden. *Shouldn't* be. Otherwise, it was like not eating what they were really eating. Perhaps the other flavors served to enhance that flavor, to give it a worthy background, to honor it."

At these words I felt again the need to look her in the teeth, as I had done earlier, when we were coming down in the bus. But at that very moment her tongue, moist with saliva, emerged from between her teeth, then immediately drew back, as if she were mentally savoring something. I realized Olivia was already imagining the supper menu.

It began, this menu, offered us by a restaurant we found among low houses with curving grilles, with a rose-colored liquid in a hand-blown glass: *sopa de camarones*—shrimp soup, that is, immeasurably hot, thanks to some variety of *chiles* we had never come upon previously, perhaps the famous *chiles jalapeños.* Then *cabrito*—roast kid—every morsel of which provoked surprise, because the teeth would encounter first a crisp bit, then one that melted in the mouth.

"You're not eating?" Olivia asked me. She seemed to concentrate only on savoring her dish, though she was very alert, as usual, while I had remained lost in thought, looking at her. It was the sensation of her teeth in my flesh that I was imagining, and I could feel her tongue lift me against the roof of her mouth, enfold me in saliva, then thrust me under the tips of the canines. I sat there facing her, but at the same time it was as if a part of me, or all of me, were contained in her mouth, crunched, torn shred by shred. The situation was not entirely passive, since while I was being chewed by her I felt also that I was acting on her, transmitting sensations that spread from the taste buds through her whole body. I was the one who aroused her every vibration— it was a reciprocal and complete relationship, which involved us and overwhelmed us.

I regained my composure; so did she. We looked

carefully at the salad of tender prickly-pear leaves (*en-salada de nopalitos*)—boiled, seasoned with garlic, coriander, red pepper, and oil and vinegar—then the pink and creamy pudding of *maguey* (a variety of agave), all accompanied by a carafe of *sangrita* and followed by coffee with cinnamon.

But this relationship between us, established exclusively through food, so much so that it could be identified in no image other than that of a meal—this relationship which in my imaginings I thought corresponded to Olivia's deepest desires—didn't please her in the slightest, and her irritation was to find its release during that same supper.

"How boring you are! How monotonous!" she began by saying, repeating an old complaint about my uncommunicative nature and my habit of giving her full responsibility for keeping the conversation alive—an argument that flared up whenever we were alone together at a restaurant table, including a list of charges whose basis in truth I couldn't help admitting but in which I also discerned the fundamental reasons for our unity as a couple; namely, that Olivia saw and knew how to catch and isolate and rapidly define many more things than I, and therefore my relationship with the world was essentially via her. "You're always sunk into yourself, unable to participate in what's going on around you, unable to put yourself out for another, never a flash of enthusiasm on your own, always ready to cast a pall on anybody else's, depressing, indifferent—" And to the inventory of my faults she added this time a new adjective, or one that to my ears now took on a new meaning: "Insipid!"

There: I was insipid, I thought, without flavor. And the Mexican cuisine, with all its boldness and imagination, was needed if Olivia was to feed on me with satisfaction. The spiciest flavors were the complement— indeed, the avenue of communication, indispensable as a loudspeaker that amplifies sounds—for Olivia to be nourished by my substance.

"I may seem insipid to you," I protested, "but there are ranges of flavor more discreet and restrained than that of red peppers. There are subtle tastes that one must know how to perceive!"

THE next morning we left Oaxaca in Salustiano's car. Our friend had to visit other provinces on the candidate's tour, and offered to accompany us for part of our itinerary. At one point on the trip he showed us some recent excavations not yet overrun by tourists. A stone statue rose barely above the level of the ground, with the unmistakable form that we had learned to recognize on the very first days of our Mexican archeological wanderings: the *chacmool*, or half-reclining human figure, in an almost Etruscan pose, with a tray resting on his belly. He looks like a rough, good-natured puppet, but it was on that tray that the victims' hearts were offered to the gods.

"Messenger of the gods—what does that mean?" I asked. I had read that definition in a guidebook. "Is he a demon sent to earth by the gods to collect the dish with the offering? Or an emissary from human beings who must go to the gods and offer them the food?"

"Who knows?" Salustiano answered, with the suspended attitude he took in the face of unanswerable questions, as if listening to the inner voices he had at his disposal, like reference books. "It could be the victim himself, supine on the altar, offering his own entrails on the dish. Or the sacrificer, who assumes the pose of the victim because he is aware that tomorrow it will be his turn. Without this reciprocity, human sacrifice would be unthinkable. All were potentially both sacrificer and victim—the victim accepted his role as victim because he had fought to capture the others as victims."

"They could be eaten because they themselves were eaters of men?" I added, but Salustiano was talking now about the serpent as symbol of the continuity of life and the cosmos.

Meanwhile I understood: my mistake with Olivia was to consider myself eaten by her, whereas I should be myself (I always had been) the one who ate her. The most appetizingly flavored human flesh belongs to the eater of human flesh. It was only by feeding ravenously on Olivia that I would cease being tasteless to her palate.

This was in my mind that evening when I sat down with her to supper. "What's wrong with you? You're odd this evening," Olivia said, since nothing ever escaped her. The dish they had served us was called *gorditas pellizcadas con manteca*—literally, "plump girls pinched with butter." I concentrated on devouring, with every meatball, the whole fragrance of Olivia—through voluptuous mastication, a vampire extraction of vital juices. But I realized that in a relationship that should have been among three terms—me, meatball, Olivia— a fourth term had intruded, assuming a dominant role: the name of the meatballs. It was the name "*gorditas pellizcadas con manteca*" that I was especially savoring and assimilating and possessing. And, in fact, the magic of that name continued affecting me even after the meal, when we retired together to our hotel room in the night. And for the first time during our Mexican journey the spell whose victims we had been was broken, and the inspiration that had blessed the finest moments of our joint life came to visit us again.

The next morning we found ourselves sitting up in our bed in the *chacmool* pose, with the dulled expression of stone statues on our faces and, on our laps, the tray with the anonymous hotel breakfast, to which we tried to add local flavors, ordering with it mangoes, papayas, cherimoyas, guayabas—fruits that conceal in the sweetness of their pulp subtle messages of asperity and sourness.

OUR journey moved into the Maya territories. The temples of Palenque emerged from the tropical forest, dominated by thick, wooded mountains: enormous ficus trees with multiple trunks like roots, lilac-colored *macuilis, aguacates*—every tree wrapped in a cloak of lianas and climbing vines and hanging plants. As I was

going down the steep stairway of the Temple of the
Inscriptions, I had a dizzy spell. Olivia, who disliked
stairs, had chosen not to follow me and had remained
with the crowd of noisy groups, loud in sound and color,
that the buses were disgorging and ingesting constantly
in the open space among the temples. By myself, I had
climbed to the Temple of the Sun, to the relief of the
jaguar sun, to the Temple of the Foliated Cross, to the
relief of the *quetzal* in profile, then to the Temple of
the Inscriptions, which involves not only climbing up
(and then down) a monumental stairway but also
climbing down (and then up) the smaller, interior staircase that leads down to the underground crypt. In the
crypt there is the tomb of the king-priest (which I had
already been able to study far more comfortably a few
days previously in a perfect facsimile at the Anthropo-
logical Museum in Mexico City), with the highly complicated carved stone slab on which you see the king
operating a science-fiction apparatus that to our eyes
resembles the sort of thing used to launch space rock-
ets, though it represents, on the contrary, the descent
of the body to the subterranean gods and its rebirth as
vegetation.

I went down, I climbed back up into the light of the
jaguar sun—into the sea of the green sap of the leaves.
The world spun, I plunged down, my throat cut by the
knife of the king-priest, down the high steps onto the
forest of tourists with super-8s and usurped, broad-
brimmed sombreros. The solar energy coursed along
dense networks of blood and chlorophyll; I was living

and dying in all the fibers of what is chewed and digested and in all the fibers that absorb the sun, consuming and digesting.

Under the thatched arbor of a restaurant on a riverbank, where Olivia had waited for me, our teeth began to move slowly, with equal rhythm, and our eyes stared into each other's with the intensity of serpents'—serpents concentrated in the ecstasy of swallowing each other in turn, as we were aware, in our turn, of being swallowed by the serpent that digests us all, assimilated ceaselessly in the process of ingestion and digestion, in the universal cannibalism that leaves its imprint on every amorous relationship and erases the lines between our bodies and *sopa de frijoles, huachinango a la vera cruzana,* and *enchiladas.*

July 19, 1982
Paris

A
KING
LISTENS

THE scepter must be held in the right hand, erect; you must never, never put it down, and for that matter you would have no place to put it: there are no tables beside the throne, or shelves, or stands to hold, say, a glass, an ashtray, a telephone. High, at the top of steep and narrow steps, the throne is isolated; if you drop any-thing, it rolls down and can never be found afterwards. God help you if the scepter slips from your grasp; you would have to rise, get down from the throne to pick it up; no one but the king may touch it. And it would hardly be a pretty sight to see a king stretched out on the floor to reach the scepter fetched up under some piece of furniture—or, when it comes to that, the crown, which could easily fall off your head if you bend over.

You can rest your forearm on the arm of the chair, so it will not tire. I am still speaking of your right arm, the one holding the scepter. As for the left, it remains

free: you can scratch yourself if you like. At times the
ermine cloak makes your neck itch, and the itch then
spreads down your back and over your whole body.
The velvet of the cushion, too, as it grows warm, pro-
duces an irritating sensation in the buttocks, the thighs.
Feel no compunction about digging your fingers in where
you itch, unfastening the gilt buckle of your big belt,
shifting your collar, your medals, the fringed epau-
lettes. You are the king; nobody can utter a word of
censure. The very idea.

The head must be held immobile; always remember
that the crown is balanced on your pate, you cannot
pull it over your ears like a cap on a windy day. The
crown rises in a dome, more voluminous than the base
that supports it, which means that its equilibrium is un-
stable: if you happen to doze off, to let your chin sink
to your chest, the crown will then go rolling down and
smash to bits, because it is fragile, especially the gold
filagree studded with diamonds. When you feel it is
about to slip, you have to be clever enough to adjust
its position with little twitches of the head; but you
must take care not to straighten up too brusquely or
you will strike the crown against the baldaquin, whose
draperies just graze it. In other words, you must maintain the regal composure that is supposed to be innate
in your person.

For that matter, what need would you have to take
all this trouble? You are the king; everything you desire
is already yours. You have only to lift a finger and you
are brought food, drink, chewing gum, toothpicks, cig-

arettes of every brand, all on a silver tray. When you feel sleepy, the throne is comfortable, overstuffed; you have only to close your eyes and relax against the back, while apparently maintaining your usual position. Whether you are asleep or awake, it is all the same: nobody notices. As for your corporal needs, it is no secret to anyone that the throne has an opening, like any self-respecting throne; twice a day they come to change the pot. More frequently, if it stinks.

In short, everything is foreordained to spare you any movement whatsoever. You would have nothing to gain by moving, and everything to lose. If you rise, if you take even a few steps, if you lose sight of the throne for an instant, who can guarantee that when you return you will not find someone else sitting on it? Perhaps someone who resembles you, identical to you. Go ahead then and try to prove you are the king, not he! A king is denoted by the fact that he is sitting on the throne, wearing the crown, holding the scepter. Now that these attributes are yours, you had better not be separated from them even for a moment.

There is the problem of stretching the legs, avoiding numbness, stiffened joints; to be sure, this is a serious inconvenience. But you can always kick, raise your knees, huddle up on the throne, sit there Turkish-fashion: naturally, for brief periods, when matters of State permit. Every evening those charged with the washing of the feet arrive and take off your boots for a quarter-hour; in the morning the deodorizing squad rubs your armpits with tufts of scented cotton.

The eventuality of your being seized with carnal desires has also been foreseen. Carefully chosen and trained court ladies, from the sturdiest to the most slender, are at your disposal, in turn, to ascend the steps of the throne and approach your timorous knees with their full skirts, gauzy and fluttering. The things that can be done, while you remain on the throne and they offer themselves frontally or from behind or at an angle, are various, and you can perform them in a few instants or, if the duties of the Realm grant you enough free time, you can linger a bit longer, say even three-quarters of an hour. In this case it is a good idea to have the curtains of the baldaquin drawn, to remove the king's intimacy from outside gazes, as the musicians play caressing melodies.

In sum, the throne, once you have been crowned, is where you had best remain seated, without moving, day and night. All your previous life has been only a waiting to become king; now you are king; you have only to reign. And what is reigning if not this long wait? Waiting for the moment when you will be deposed, when you will have to take leave of the throne, the scepter, the crown, and your head.

THE hours are slow to pass; in the throne room the lamplight is always the same. You listen to time flowing by: a buzz like a wind; the wind blows along the corridors of the palace or in the depths of your ear. Kings do not have watches: it is assumed that they are the ones who govern the flow of time; submission to the rules of a mechanical device would be incompatible with regal majesty. The minutes' uniform expanse threatens to bury you like an avalanche of sand: but you know how to elude it. You have only to prick up your ears in order to recognize the sounds of the palace, which change from hour to hour: in the morning the trumpet blares for the flag-raising on the tower; the trucks of the royal household unload hampers and casks in the courtyard of the stores; the maidservants beat the carpets on the railing of the loggia; at evening the gates creak as they are closed, a clatter rises from the kitchens, from the stables an occasional whinny indicates that it is currying time.

The palace is a clock: its ciphered sounds follow the course of the sun; invisible arrows point to the change of the guard on the ramparts with a scuffle of hob-nailed boots, a slamming of rifle-butts, answered by the crunch of gravel under the tanks kept ready on the forecourt. If the sounds are repeated in the customary order, at the proper intervals, you can be reassured, your reign is in no danger: for the moment, for this hour, for this day still.

Sunk on your throne, you raise your hand to your ear, you shift the draperies of the baldaquin so that they will not muffle the slightest murmur, the faintest echo. For you the days are a succession of sounds, some distinct, some almost imperceptible; you have learned to distinguish them, to evaluate their provenance and their distance; you know their order, you know how long the pauses last; you are already awaiting every reso-

nance or creak or clink that is about to reach your tym-
panum; you anticipate it in your imagination; if it is
late in being produced, you grow impatient. Your anxiety is not allayed until the thread of hearing is knotted
again, until the weft of thoroughly familiar sounds is
mended at the place where a gap seemed to have opened.

Vestibules, stairways, loggias, corridors of the palace
have high, vaulted ceilings; every footstep, every click
of a lock, every sneeze echoes, rebounds, is propagated
horizontally along a suite of communicating rooms, halls,
colonnades, service entries, and also vertically, through
stairwells, cavities, skylights, conduits, flues, the shafts
of dumbwaiters; and all the acoustical routes converge
on the throne room. Into the great lake of silence where
you are floating rivers of air empty, stirred by inter-
mittent vibrations. Alert, intent, you intercept them and
decipher them. The palace is all whorls, lobes: it is a
great ear, whose anatomy and architecture trade names
and functions: pavilions, ducts, shells, labyrinths. You
are crouched at the bottom, in the innermost zone of
the palace-ear, of your own ear; the palace is the ear of
the king.

HERE the walls have ears. Spies are stationed behind
every drapery, curtain, arras. Your spies, the agents of
your secret service: their assignment is to draft detailed
reports on the palace conspiracies. The court teems with
enemies, to such an extent that it is increasingly difficult to tell them from friends; it is known for sure that
the conspiracy that will dethrone you will be made up

of your ministers and officials. And you know that every secret service has been infiltrated by agents of the opposing secret service. Perhaps all the agents in your pay work also for the conspirators, are themselves conspirators; and thus you are obliged to continue paying them, to keep them quiet as long as possible.

Voluminous bundles of secret reports are turned out daily by electronic machines and laid at your feet on the steps of the throne. It is pointless for you to read them: your spies can only confirm the existence of the conspiracies, justifying the necessity of your espionage; and at the same time they must deny any immediate danger, to prove that their spying is effective. No one, for that matter, thinks you must read the reports delivered to you; the light in the throne room is inadequate for reading, and the assumption is that a king need not read anything, the king already knows what he has to know. To be reassured you have only to hear the clicking of the electronic machines coming from the secret services' offices during the eight hours established by the schedule. A swarm of operators feeds new data into the memory banks, follows complicated tabulations on the screens, pulls from the printers new reports, which are always the same report, repeated day after day with minimal variations regarding rain or fair weather. With minimal variations the same printers turn out the secret bulletins of the conspirators, the order of the day for the mutinies, the detailed plans for your deposition and execution.

You can read them, if you wish. Or pretend to have

read them. What the spies' eavesdropping records, whether at your command or your enemies', is the maximum that can be translated into the code formulas, inserted into programs specifically devised to produce secret reports conforming to the official models. Threatening or comforting as it may be, the future that unfolds on those pages no longer belongs to you, it does not resolve your uncertainty. What you want revealed is something quite different, the fear and the hope that keep you awake, holding your breath, in the night: what your ears try to learn, about yourself, about your fate.

THIS palace, when you ascended the throne, at the very moment when it became your palace, became alien to you. Advancing at the head of the coronation procession, you walked through it for the last time, amid torches and flabella, before retiring to this hall which it is neither prudent nor in accord with royal protocol for you to leave. What would a king do, roaming through corridors, offices, kitchens? There is no longer any place for you in the palace, save this hall.

The recollection of the other rooms, as you saw them the last time, quickly faded in your memory: and for that matter, bedecked as they were for the festivity, they were unrecognizable places, you would have got lost in them.

Sharper in your memory are certain glimpses remaining from the battle, when you moved to attack the palace at the head of your then loyal followers (who are now surely preparing to betray you): balustrades shattered by mortar explosions, breaches in the walls singed by fires, pocked by volleys of bullets. You can no longer think of it as the same palace in which you are seated on the throne; if you were to find yourself in it again, that would be a sign that the cycle has completed its course and your ruin is dragging you off, in your turn.

Still earlier, in the years you spent plotting at the court of your predecessor, you saw yet another palace, because certain apartments and not others were assigned to staff of your rank, and because your ambitions focused on the transformations you would bring about in the appearance of those places once you became king. The first order every new king issues, the moment he is installed on the throne, is to alter the arrangement and purpose of every room, the furniture, the wall-hangings, the plaster decoration. You did this, too, and you thought you would thus mark your real possession. On the contrary, you simply cast more memories in the grinder of oblivion, from which nothing is ever recovered.

To be sure, the palace contains some so-called historic chambers, which you would like to see again, even though they have been redone from top to bottom, to give them back the antique aspect lost with the passing years. But those rooms have recently been opened to tourists. You must stay well away from them; curled up on your throne, you recognize in your calendar of sounds the visiting days by the noise of the buses that stop in the plaza, the blathering of the guides, the chorus of amazed exclamations in various languages. Even on the days when the rooms are closed, you are formally advised against venturing there: you would stumble over the cleaning squad's brooms, the buckets, the drums of detergent. At night you would be lost, blocked by the reddening eyes of the alarm signals that bar your path, and in the morning you would find yourself trapped by parties armed with video cameras, regiments of old ladies with false teeth, wearing blue veils over their permanents, and obese gentlemen with flowered shirts hanging outside their trousers and with broad-brimmed straw hats on their heads.

WHILE your palace remains unknown to you and unknowable, you can try to reconstruct it bit by bit, locating every shuffle, every cough at a point in space, imagining walls around each acoustical sign, ceilings, pavements, giving form to the void in which the sounds spread and to the obstacles they encounter, allowing the sounds themselves to prompt the images. A silvery tinkle is not simply a spoon that has fallen from the saucer where it was balanced, but is also a corner of a table covered with a linen cloth with lace fringe, in the light from a high window over which boughs of wistaria hang; a soft thud is not only a cat that has leaped upon a mouse, but is also a damp, moldy space beneath some steps, closed off by planks bristling with nails.

The palace is a construction of sounds that expands one moment and contracts the next, tightens like a tangle of chains. You can move through it, guided by the echoes, localizing creaks, clangs, curses, pursuing breaths, rustles, grumbles, gurgles.

The palace is the body of the king. Your body sends you mysterious messages, which you receive with fear, with anxiety. In an unknown part of this body, a menace is lurking, your death is already stationed there; the signals that reach you warn you perhaps of a danger buried in your own interior. The body seated askew on the throne is no longer yours, you have been deprived of its use ever since the crown encircled your head; now your person is spread out through this dark, alien residence that speaks to you in riddles. But has anything really changed? Even before, you knew little or nothing about what you were. And you were afraid of it, as you are now.

The palace is a weft of regular sounds, always the same, like the heart's beat, from which other sounds stand out, discordant, unexpected. A door slams. Where? Someone runs down steps, a stifled cry is heard. Long, tense minutes pass. A prolonged, shrill whistle resounds, perhaps from a window in the tower. Another whistle replies, from below. Then silence.

Does some story link one sound to another? You cannot help looking for a meaning, concealed perhaps not in single, isolated noises but between them, in the pauses that separate them. And if there is a story, does that story concern you? Will some series of consequences involve you finally? Or is it simply another indifferent episode among the many that make up the daily life of the palace? Every story you seem to divine brings you back to yourself, nothing happens in the palace unless the king has some part in it, active or passive. From the faintest clue you can derive an augury of your fate.

Perhaps the threat comes more from the silences than from the sounds. How many hours has it been since you heard the changing of the sentries? And what if the squad of guards faithful to you has been captured by the conspirators? Why has the familiar banging of pots not been heard from the kitchens? Have your trusted cooks perhaps been replaced by a team of killers, accustomed to sheathing all their actions in silence, poisoners now silently steeping the foods in cyanide. . . ?

Perhaps danger lurks in regularity itself. The trumpeter sounds the usual blast at the exact hour, as on every other day; but do you not sense that he is doing this with too much precision? Do you not catch a strange insistence in the rolling of the drums, an excess of zeal? The patrol's marching tread that reechoes along its round seems today to beat a lugubrious cadence, almost like a firing squad's. . . . The tracks of the tanks pass over the gravel almost without a creak, as if the mechanisms had been oiled more abundantly than usual: perhaps in the prospect of a battle?

Perhaps the troops of the guard are no longer those who were faithful to you. . . . Or perhaps, without their being replaced, they have gone over to the side of the conspirators. . . . Perhaps everything continues as before, but the palace is already in the hands of the usurpers; they have not arrested you yet because, after all, you no longer count for anything. They have forgotten you on a throne that is no longer a throne. The regular unfolding of palace life is a sign that the coup has taken place, a new king sits on a new throne, your sentence has been pronounced and it is so irrevocable that there is no need to carry it out in a hurry. . . .

STOP raving. Everything heard moving in the palace corresponds precisely to the rules you have laid down: the army obeys your orders like a prompt machine: the ritual of the palace does not allow the slightest variation in setting and clearing the table, in drawing the curtains or unrolling the ceremonial carpets according to the instructions received; the radio programs are those you decreed once and for all. The situation is in your grip; nothing eludes your will or your control. Even the frog that croaks in the basin, even the uproar of the children playing blind-man's-buff, even the old chamberlain's sprawl down the stairs: everything corresponds to your plan, everything has been thought out by you, decided, pondered, before it became audible to your ear. Not even a fly buzzes here if you do not wish it.

But perhaps you have never been so close to losing everything as you are now, when you think you have everything in your grip. The responsibility of conceiving the palace in its every detail, of containing it in your mind, subjects you to an exhausting strain. The obstinacy on which power is based is never so fragile as in the moment of its triumph.

NEAR the throne there is an angle of the wall from which every now and then you hear a kind of reverberation:

distant blows, like knocking at a door. Is there someone rapping on the other side of the wall? But perhaps
it is more a pilaster than a wall, a support that juts out,
a hollow column, perhaps a vertical duct that runs
through all the floors of the palace from the cellars to
the roof, a flue, for example, that begins at the fur-
naces. Along this route sounds are transmitted through
the entire height of the building; at one point of the
palace, there is no knowing on which floor, but surely
above or below the throne room something is striking
the duct. Something or someone. Someone is striking
cadenced blows with his fist; the muffled reverberation
suggests that the raps come from far off. Blows that
emerge from a dark profundity, yes, from below; a
knocking that rises from underground. Are these raps
signals?

Stretching out one arm, you can bang your fist against
the corner. You repeat the blows as you have just heard
them. Silence. Ah, there! they are heard again. The order of the pauses and the frequence are slightly changed.
You repeat this time, too. Wait. Once more, you do
not have to wait long for a reply. Have you established
a dialogue?

For a dialogue you must know the language. A series
of raps, one after the other, a pause, then more, isolated raps: can these signals be translated into a code?
Is someone forming letters, words? Does someone want
to communicate with you, does he have urgent things
to say to you? Try the simplest key: one rap, *a*; two
raps, *b*. . . . Or try Morse, make an effort to distin-

guish short sounds and long sounds. . . . At times it
seems to you that the transmitted message has a rhythm,
as in a musical phrase: this would also prove a wish to
attract your attention, to communicate, to speak to you.
. . . But this is not enough for you: if the raps follow
one another with regularity they must form a word, a
sentence. . . . And now you would already like to im-
pose on the bare drip of sounds your desire for reassuring words: "Your Majesty . . . we . . . your loyal
subjects . . . will foil all plots . . . long life . . ." Is
this what they are saying to you? Is this what you manage to decipher, trying to apply all conceivable codes?
No, nothing of the sort comes out. If anything, the
message that emerges is entirely different, more on the
order of: "Bastard dog usurper . . . vengeance . . .
you will be overthrown. . . . "

Calm down. Perhaps it is all your imagination. Only
chance combines the letters and words in this way. Perhaps these are not even signals: it could be the slamming of a door in a draft, or a child bouncing his ball,
or someone hammering nails. Nails . . . "The coffin
. . . your coffin . . ."—now the raps form these
words—"I will emerge from this coffin . . . and you
will enter it . . . buried alive . . ." Words without
meaning, after all. Only your imagination imposes raving words on those formless reverberations.

You might as well imagine that when you rap your
knuckles on the wall, drumming at random, someone
else, listening God knows where in the palace, believes
he can understand words, sentences. Try it. Without

giving it any thought. Now what are you doing? Why
do you concentrate so, as if you were spelling, making
words? What message do you think you are sending
down this wall? "You, too, usurper before me . . . I
have defeated you . . . I could have killed you . . . "
What are you doing? Are you trying to justify yourself
to an invisible sound? Whom are you entreating? "I
spared your life. . . . If your turn comes . . . remember . . ." Who do you think there is down below,
striking the wall? Do you think your predecessor is still
alive, the king you drove from the throne, from this
throne where you are sitting? Is he the prisoner you
had sealed up in the deepest cell of the palace?

You spend every night listening to the underground
tom-tom, trying in vain to decipher its messages. But
you harbor the suspicion that it is only a noise you
have in your ears, the throbbing of your heart in up-
heaval, or the recollection of a rhythm that surfaces in
your memory and reawakens fears, remorse. In train
journeys at night the rumble of the wheels, always the
same, is transformed, as you doze, into repeated words;
it becomes a kind of monotonous chant. It is possible,
nay, probable, that every undulation of sounds is transformed, in your ear, into the lament of a prisoner, the
curses of your victims, the ominous panting of your
enemies whom you cannot manage to kill. . . .

You are wise to listen, not to let your attention lapse
even for an instant; but you must be convinced of this:
it is yourself you hear, it is within you that the ghosts

acquire voices. Something you are incapable of saying even to yourself is trying painfully to make itself heard. . . . You are not convinced? You want absolute proof that what you hear comes from within you, not from outside?

Absolute proof you will never have. Because it is true that the dungeons of the palace are filled with prisoners, supporters of the deposed sovereign, courtiers suspected of disloyalty, strangers caught in the roundups your police carry out periodically as a precautionary intimidation, and then the victims end up forgotten in high-security cells. . . . Since all these people keep shaking their chains day and night, or rattle their spoons against the bars, chanting protests, striking up seditious songs, it would be only natural if some echo of their din came all the way up to you, even though you have had walls and floors soundproofed, and have sheathed this hall with heavy draperies. It is not impossible that from those very dungeons there comes what seemed to you before a cadenced rapping but now has become a kind of deep, grim thunder. Every palace stands on cellars where someone is buried alive or where some dead man cannot find peace. You need not bother covering your ears with your hands: you will go on hearing them all the same.

Do not become obsessed with the noises of the palace, unless you wish to be snared in them as in a trap. Go out! Run away! Rove! Outside the palace spreads the city, the capital of the realm, your realm! You have become king not to possess this sad, dark palace, but the city, various and pied, clamorous, with its thousand voices!

The city is stretched out in the night, curled up, it sleeps and snores, dreams and growls: patches of shadow and light shift every time it rolls over on this side or on that. Every morning the bells ring festively, or warningly, or in alarm: they send messages, but you can never trust what they really want to tell you. With their tolling for the dead you hear, mingled by the wind, some lively dance music; in the festive pealing, an explosion of infuriated voices. It is the breathing of the city to which you must listen, a breathing that can be labored and gasping or calm and deep.

The city is a distant rumble at the bottom of the ear, a hum of voices, a buzz of wheels. When in the palace all is still, the city moves, the wheels run through the streets, the streets run like the spokes of wheels, disks spin on gramophones, a needle scratches an old record, the music comes and goes, in gusts, it oscillates, down in the rumbling groove of the streets, or it rises high with the wind that spins the vanes of the chimneys. The city is a wheel whose hub is the place where you remain immobile, listening.

In summer the city comes through the open windows of the palace; it flies from all its own open windows, with its voices, outbursts of laughter and of tears, chatter of pneumatic drills, squawking of transistors. It is pointless for you to peer out from the balcony; seeing the roofs from above, you would recognize nothing of the streets you have not walked along since the day of your coronation, when the procession advanced among banners and decorations and lines of guards, and everything seemed even then already unrecognizable, distant.

The cool of the evening does not arrive as far as the throne room, but you recognize it from the summer-evening hum that does reach you even here. You might as well give up the idea of looking out from the balcony: you would gain nothing but mosquito bites, nothing that is not already contained in this roar, like that of a shell held to the ear. The city holds the roar of an ocean as in the whorls of the shell, or of the ear: if you concentrate on listening to the waves, you no longer know what is palace and what is city, ear, shell.

Among the sounds of the city you recognize every now and then a chord, a sequence of notes, a tune: blasts of fanfare, chanting of processions, choruses of schoolchildren, funeral marches, revolutionary songs intoned by a parade of demonstrators, anthems in your honor sung by the troops who break up the demonstration, trying to drown out the voices of your opponents, dance tunes that the loudspeaker of a nightclub plays at top volume to convince everyone that the city continues its happy life, dirges of women mourning someone killed in the riots. This is the music you hear; but can it be called music? From every shard of sound you continue to gather signals, information, clues, as if in this city all those who play or sing or put on disks wanted only to transmit precise, unequivocal messages to you. Since you mounted the throne, it is not music you listen to, but only the confirmation of how music is used: in the rites of high society, or to entertain the populace, to safeguard traditions, culture, fashion. Now you ask yourself what listening used to mean to you, when you listened to music for the sole pleasure of penetrating the design of the notes.

Once, to be happy, you had only to sketch a "tralalalà" with your lips, or with your mind, imitating the tune you had caught, in a simple little song or in a complex symphony. Now you try going "tralalalà," but nothing happens: no tune comes into your mind.

THERE was a voice, a song, a woman's voice that from time to time the breeze carried all the way up here to you from some open window; there was a love song that on summer nights the air brought you in bursts, and the moment you seemed to have grasped some note of it, it was already lost, and you were never sure you had really heard it and had not simply imagined it, desired to hear it, the dream of a woman's voice singing in the nightmare of your long insomnia. This is what you were waiting for, quiet and alert: it is no longer fear that makes you prick up your ears. You have begun to hear again this singing that reaches you with every note distinct, every timbre and color, from the city that has been abandoned by all music.

It has been a long time since you felt yourself attracted by something, perhaps since the time when all your powers became concentrated on conquering the throne. But all you remember now of the yearning that devoured you is your persistence against the enemies to overcome, which did not allow you to desire or imag-

ine anything else. Even then it was a thought of death
that accompanied you, day and night, as it does now,
while you peer at the city in the darkness and silence
of the curfew you have imposed to defend yourself
against the revolt that is hatching; and you follow the
tramp of the patrols on their rounds through the empty
streets. And when in the darkness a woman's voice is
released in singing, invisible at the sill of an unlighted
window, then all of a sudden thoughts of life come back
to you: your desires find an object. What is it? Not
that song, which you must have heard all too many
times, not that woman, whom you have never seen:
you are attracted by that voice as a voice, as it offers
itself in song.

THAT voice comes certainly from a person, unique, inimitable like every person; a voice, however, is not a
person, it is something suspended in the air, detached
from the solidity of things. The voice, too, is unique
and inimitable, but perhaps in a different way from a
person: they might not resemble each other, voice and
person. Or else, they could resemble each other in a
secret way, not perceptible at first: the voice could be
the equivalent of the hidden and most genuine part of
the person. Is it a bodiless you that listens to that bodiless voice? In that case, whether you actually hear it or
merely remember it or imagine it makes no difference.

And yet, you want it to be truly your ear that per-
ceives that voice, so what attracts you is not only a
memory or a fancy but the throbbing of a throat of

flesh. A voice means this: there is a living person, throat, chest, feelings, who sends into the air this voice, different from all other voices. A voice involves the throat, saliva, infancy, the patina of experienced life, the mind's intentions, the pleasure of giving a personal form to sound waves. What attracts you is the pleasure this voice puts into existing: into existing as voice; but this pleasure leads you to imagine how this person might be different from every other person, as the voice is different.

Are you trying to imagine the woman who sings? But no matter what image you try to attribute to her in your imagination, the image-voice will always be richer. You surely do not wish to lose any of the possibilities it contains; and so it is best for you to stick to the voice, resist the temptation to run outside the palace and explore the city street by street until you find the woman who is singing.

But it is impossible to restrain you. There is a part of yourself that is running toward the unknown voice. Infected by its pleasure in making itself heard, you would like your listening to be heard by her, you would like to be voice, too, heard by her as you hear her.

Too bad you cannot sing. If you had known how to sing, perhaps your life would have been different, happier; or sad with a different sadness, a harmonious melancholy. Perhaps you would not have felt the need to become king. Now you would not find yourself here, on this creaking throne, peering at shadows.

Buried deep within yourself perhaps your true voice exists, the song that cannot break free of your clenched throat, from your lips parched and taut. Or else your voice wanders, scattered, through the city, timbres and tones disseminated in the buzzing. The man you are or have been or could be, the you that no one knows, would be revealed in that voice.

Try, concentrate, summon your secret strength. Now! No, that will not do. Try again, do not be disheartened. Ah, there! Now: miracle! You cannot believe your ears! Whose is this voice with the warm, baritone timbre that rises, finds its pitch, harmonizes with the silvery flashes of her voice? Who is singing this duet with her as if they were two complementary and symmetrical faces of the same vocal will? It is you who are singing, no doubt about it: this is your voice, which you can listen to at last without alienation or irritation.

But where are you able to find and produce these notes, if your chest remains contracted and your teeth clenched? You are convinced that the city is nothing but a physical extension of her person; and where should the king's voice come from then if not from the very heart of his kingdom's capital? With the same sharpness of ear that has enabled you to catch and follow until this moment the song of that unknown woman, now you collect the hundred fragments of sound that, united, compose an unmistakable voice, the voice that alone is yours.

There, dismiss every intrusion and distraction from your hearing. Concentrate: you must catch the wom-

an's voice calling you and your voice calling her, together, in the same intention of listening (or would you
call it the vision of your ear?). Now! No, not yet. Do
not give up. Try again. In another moment her voice
and yours will answer each other and merge to such a
degree that you will no longer be able to tell them
apart. . . .

But too many sounds intrude, frantic, piercing, fe-
rocious: her voice disappears, stifled by the roar of death
that invades the outside, or that perhaps reechoes inside
you. You have lost her, you are lost; the part of you
projected into the space of sounds now runs through
the streets among the curfew patrols. The life of voices
was a dream, perhaps it lasted only a few seconds, as
dreams last, while outside the nightmare continues.

AND yet, you are the king: if you seek a woman who
lives in your capital, recognizable by her voice, you
must be quite capable of finding her. Unleash your spies,
give orders to search all the streets and all the houses.
But who knows that voice? Only you. No one but you
can carry out this search. And so, when a desire to be
fulfilled presents itself to you at last, you realize that
being king is of no use for anything.

Wait, you must not lose heart immediately; a king
has many resources. Is it possible that you cannot de-
vise a system to obtain what you want? You could an-
nounce a singing contest: by order of the king all female
subjects of the realm who have a pleasant singing voice
would present themselves at the palace. It would be,

even more important, a clever political move, to soothe people's spirits in a period of unrest, and strengthen the bonds between citizenry and crown. You can easily imagine the scene: in this hall, festively decorated, a platform, an orchestra, an audience made up of the leading figures of the court, and you, impassive, on the throne, listening to every high note, every trill with the attention suitable in an impartial judge, until suddenly you raise your scepter and declare: "She is the one!"

How could you fail to recognize her? No voice could be less like those that usually perform for the king, in the halls illuminated by crystal chandeliers, among the potted plants with broad, flat palm-like leaves. You have been present at many concerts in your honor on the dates of glorious anniversaries; every voice aware of being heard by the king takes on a cold enamel, a glassy smugness. That one, on the contrary, was a voice that came from the shadow, happy to display itself without emerging from the darkness that hid it, casting a bridge toward every presence enfolded in the same darkness.

But are you sure that, before the steps of the throne, it would be the same voice? That it would not try to imitate the intonation of the court singers? That it would not be confused with the many voices you have become accustomed to hearing, with condescending approbation, as you follow the flight of a fly?

The only way to impel her to reveal herself would be an encounter with your true voice, with that ghost of your voice that you summoned up from the city's tem-

pest of sounds. It would suffice for you to sing, to release that voice you have always hidden from everyone,
and she would immediately recognize you for the man
you really are, and she would join her voice, her real
voice, to yours.

Then, ah!, an exclamation of surprise would spread
through the court: "His Majesty is singing. . . . Listen
to how His Majesty sings. . . . " But the composure
which is proper in listening to the king, whatever he
says or does, would soon take over. Faces and gestures
would express a complaisant and measured approval, as
if to say: "His Majesty is graciously favoring us with a
song. . . . " and all would agree that a vocal display is
one of the sovereign's prerogatives (provided that they
can then cover you with whispered ridicule and
insults).

In short, it would be all very well for you to sing:
no one would hear you, they would not hear you, your
song, your voice. They would be listening to the king,
in the way a king must be listened to, receiving what
comes from above and has no meaning beyond the un-
changing relationship between him who is above and
those who are below. Even she, the sole addressee of
your song, could not hear you: yours would not be the
voice she hears; she would listen to the king, her body
frozen in a curtsey, with the smile prescribed by protocol masking a preconceived rejection.

YOUR every attempt to get out of the cage is destined
to fail: it is futile to seek yourself in a world that does

not belong to you, that perhaps does not exist. For you there is only the palace, the great reechoing vaults, the sentries' watches, the tanks that crunch the gravel, the hurried footsteps on the staircase which each time could be those announcing your end. These are the only signs through which the world speaks to you; do not let your attention stray from them even for an instant; the moment you are distracted, this space you have constructed around yourself to contain and watch over your fears will be rent, torn to pieces.

Is it impossible for you? Are your ears deafened by new, unusual sounds? Are you no longer able to tell the uproar outside from that inside the palace? Perhaps there is no longer an inside and an outside: while you were intent on listening to voices, the conspirators have exploited the lapse of vigilance in order to unleash the revolt.

Around you there is no longer a palace, there is the night filled with cries and shots. Where are you? Are you still alive? Have you eluded the assassins who have burst into the throne room? Did the secret stairway afford you an avenue of escape?

The city has exploded in flames and shouts. The night has exploded, turned inside out. Darkness and silence plunge into themselves and throw out their reverse of fire and screams. The city crumples like a burning page. Run, without crown, without scepter; no one will realize that you are the king. There is no night darker than a night of fires. There is no man more alone than one running in the midst of a howling mob.

The night of the countryside keeps watch over the throes of the city. An alarm spreads with the shrieks of the nocturnal birds, but the farther it moves from the walls, the more it is lost among the rustlings of the usual darkness: the wind in the leaves, the flowing of the streams, the croaking of the frogs. Space expands in the noisy silence of the night, where events are dots of sudden din that flare up and die away; the crack of a broken bough, the squeaking of a dormouse when a snake comes into his hole, two cats in love, fighting, a sliding of pebbles beneath your fugitive steps.

You pant, you pant and under the dark sky only your panting is heard, the crackle of leaves beneath your stumbling feet. Why are the frogs quiet now? No, there they begin again. A dog barks. . . . Stop. The dogs answer one another from a distance. For some time you have been walking in thick darkness, you have lost all notion of where you might be. You prick up your ears. There is someone else panting like you. Where?

The night is all breathing. A low wind has risen as if from the grass. The crickets never stop, on all sides. If you isolate one sound from another, it seems to burst forth suddenly, very distinct; but it was also there before, hidden among the other sounds.

You also were there, before. And now? You could not answer. You do not know which of these breaths is yours. You no longer know how to listen. There is no longer anyone listening to anyone else. Only the night listens to itself.

Your footsteps reecho. Above your head there is no

longer the sky. The wall you touch was covered with moss, with mold; now there is rock around you, bare stone. If you call, your voice also rebounds. Where? "Ohooo . . . Ohooo . . . " Perhaps you have ended up in a cave: an interminable cavern, an underground passage. . . .

For years you have had such tunnels dug under the palace, under the city, with branches leading into the open country. . . . You wanted to assure yourself the possibility of moving everywhere without being seen; you felt you could dominate your kingdom only from the bowels of the earth. Then you let the excavations crumble in ruins. And here you are, taking refuge in your lair. Or caught in your trap. You ask yourself if you will ever find the way to go out of here. Go out: where?

Knocking. In the stone. Muffled. Cadenced. Like a signal! Where does the rapping come from? You know that cadence. It is the prisoner's call! Answer. Rap on the wall yourself. Shout. If you remember rightly, the tunnel communicates with the cells of the political prisoners. . . .

He does not know who you are: liberator or jailer? Or perhaps one who has become lost underground, like him, cut off from the news of the city and of the battle on which his fate depends?

If he is wandering outside his cell, this is a sign that they came to remove his chains, to throw open the bars. They said to him: "The usurper has fallen! You will return to your throne! You will regain possession of

the palace!" Then something must have gone wrong.
An alarm, a counterattack by the royal troops, and the
liberators ran off along the tunnels, leaving him alone.
Naturally he got lost. Under these stone vaults no light
arrives, no echo of what is happening up above.

Now you will be able to speak to each other, to recognize your voices. Will you tell him who you are?
Will you tell him that you have recognized him as the
man you have kept in prison for so many years? The
man you heard cursing your name, swearing to avenge
himself? Now you are both lost underground, and you
do not know which of you is king and which, prisoner.
It almost seems to you that, however it turns out,
nothing changes: in this cellar you seem to have been
sealed forever, sending out signals. . . . It seems to
you that your fate has always been in suspense, like
his. One of you will remain down here. . . . The
other . . .

But perhaps he, down here, has always felt that he
was up above, on the throne, with the crown on his
head, and with the scepter. And you? Did you not feel
always a prisoner? How can a dialogue be established
between the two of you if each thinks he hears, not the
words of the other, but his own words, repeated by the
echo?

For one of you the hour of rescue is approaching,
for the other, ruin. And yet that anxiety that never
abandoned you seems now to have vanished. You listen
to the echoes and the rustlings with no further need to
separate them and decipher them, as if they made up a

piece of music. A music that brings back to your memory the voice of the unknown woman. But are you remembering it or do you really hear it? Yes, it is she, it is her voice that forms that tune like a call under the rock vaults. She might also be lost, in this night like the world's end. Answer her, make yourself heard, send her a call, so that she can find her way in the darkness and join you. Why do you remain silent? Now, of all times, have you lost your voice?

There, another call rises from the darkness, at the point from which the prisoner's words came. It is an easily recognized call, which answers the woman, it is *your* voice, the voice you created to reply to her, drawing it from the dust of the city sounds, the voice you sent toward her from the silence of the throne room! The prisoner is singing your song, as if he had never done anything but sing it, as if it had never been sung by anyone else. . . .

She replies, in her turn. The two voices move toward each other, become superimposed, blend, as you had already heard them joined in the night of the city, certain that it was you singing with her. Now surely she has reached him, you hear their voices, your voices, going off together. It is useless for you to try to follow them: they are becoming a murmur, a whisper; they vanish.

IF you raise your eyes, you will see a glow. Above your head the imminent morning is brightening the sky: that breath against your face is the wind stirring the leaves.

You are outside again, the dogs are barking, the birds wake, the colors return on the world's surface, things reoccupy space, living beings again give signs of life. And surely you are also here, in the midst of it all, in the teeming noises that rise on all sides, in the buzz of the electric current, the throb of the pistons, the clank of gears. Somewhere, in a fold of the earth, the city is reawakening, with a slamming, a hammering, a creaking that grows louder. Now a noise, a rumble, a roar occupies all space, absorbs all sighs, calls, sobs. . . .

August 1, 1984
Rome

THE
NAME,
THE
NOSE

EPIGRAPHS in an undecipherable language, half their letters rubbed away by the sand-laden wind: this is what you will be, O *parfumeries*, for the noseless man of the future. You will still open your doors to us, your carpets will still muffle our footsteps, you will receive us in your jewel-box space, with no jutting corners, the walls of lacquered wood, and shopgirls or patronnes, colorful and soft as artificial flowers, will let their plump arms, wielding atomizers, graze us, or the hem of their skirts, as they stand tip-toe on stools, reaching upwards. But the phials, the ampules, the jars with their spire-like or cut-glass stoppers will weave in vain from shelf to shelf their network of harmonies, assonances, dissonances, counterpoints, modulations, cadenzas: our deaf nostrils will no longer catch the notes of their scale. We will not distinguish musk from verbena: amber and mignonette, bergamot and bitter-almond will remain mute, sealed in the calm slumber of their bottles. When the olfactory alphabet, which made them so many words in a precious lexicon, is forgotten, perfumes will be left speechless, inarticulate, illegible.

How different were the vibrations a great *parfumerie* could once stir in the spirit of a man of the world, as in the days when my carriage would stop, with a sharp tug at the reins, at a famous sign on the Champs-Elysées, and I would hurriedly get out and enter that mirrored gallery, dropping with one movement my cloak, top hat, cane, and gloves into the hands of the girls who hastened to receive them, while Madame Odile rushed toward me as if she were flying on her frills.

"Monsieur de Saint-Caliste! What a pleasant surprise! What can we offer you? A cologne? An essence of vetivert? A pomade for curling the moustache? Or a lotion to restore the hair's natural ebony hue?"

And she would flicker her lashes, her lips forming a sly smile. "Or do you wish to make an addition to the list of presents that my delivery boys carry each week, discreetly, in your name, to addresses both illustrious and obscure, scattered throughout Paris? Is it a new conquest you are about to confide in your devoted Madame Odile?"

Overcome with agitation as I was, I remained silent, writhing, while the girls already began to concern themselves with me. One slipped the gardenia from my buttonhole so that its fragrance, however faint, would not disturb my perception of the scents; another girl

drew my silk handkerchief from my pocket so it would
be ready to receive the sample drops from which I was
to choose; a third sprinkled my waistcoat with rose
water, to neutralize the stench of my cigar; a fourth
dabbled odorless lacquer on my moustache, so it would
not become impregnated with the various essences,
confusing my nostrils.

And Madame went on: "I see! A great passion! Ah!
I've been expecting this for some time, Monsieur! You
can hide nothing from me! Is she a lady of high degree?
A reigning queen of the Comédie? Or the Variétés? Or
did you make a carefree excursion into the demi-monde
and fall into the trap of sentiment? But, first of all, in
which category would you place her: the jasmine fam-
ily, the fruit blossoms, the piercing scents, or the Oriental? Tell me, *mon chou!*"

And one of her shopgirls, Martine, was already tick-
ling the tip of my ear with her finger wet with patchou-
li (pressing the sting of her breast, at the same time,
beneath my armpit), and Charlotte was extending her
arm, perfumed with orris, for me to sniff (in the same
fashion, on other occasions, I had examined a whole
sampler, arrayed over her body), and Sidonie blew on
my hand, to evaporate the drop of eglantine she had
put there (between her parted lips I could glimpse her
little teeth, whose bites I knew so well), and another,
whom I had never seen, a new girl (whom I merely
grazed with an absent pinch, preoccupied as I was),
aimed an atomizer at me, pressing its bulb, as if inviting
me to an amorous skirmish.

"No, Madame, that's not it, that's not it at all," I managed to say. "What I am looking for is not the perfume suited to a lady I know. It is the lady I must find! A lady of whom I know nothing—save her perfume!" At moments like these Madame Odile's methodical genius is at its best: only the sternest mental order allows one to rule a world of impalpable effluvia. "We shall proceed by elimination," she said, turning grave. "Is there a hint of cinnamon? Does it contain musk? Is it violet-like? Or almond?"

But how could I put into words the languid, fierce sensation I had felt the previous night, at a masked ball, when my mysterious partner for the waltz, with a lazy movement, had loosened the gauzy scarf which separated her white shoulder from my moustache, and a streaked, rippling cloud had assailed my nostrils, as if I were breathing in the soul of a tigress?

"It's a different perfume, quite different, Madame Odile, unlike any of those you mention!"

The girls were already climbing to the highest shelves, carefully handing one another fragile jars, removing the stoppers for barely a second, as if afraid the air might contaminate the essences in them.

"This heliotrope," Madam Odile told me, "is used by only four women in all Paris: the Duchesse de Clignancourt, the Marquise de Menilmontant, the wife of Coulommiers the cheese-manufacturer, and his mistress. . . . They send me this rosewood every month especially for the wife of the Tsar's Ambassador. . . . Here is a potpourri I prepare for only two customers:

the Princess of Baden-Holstein and Carole, the cour-
tesan. . . . This artemisia? I remember the names of all
the ladies who have bought it once, but never a second
time. It apparently has a depressant effect on men."

What I required of Madame Odile's specific experience was precisely this: to give a name to an olfactory
sensation I could neither forget nor hold in my memory without its slowly fading. I had to expect as much:
even the perfumes of memory evaporate: each new scent
I was made to sniff, as it imposed its diversity, its own
powerful presence, made still vaguer the recollection of
that absent perfume, reduced it to a shadow.

"No, it was sharper . . . I mean fresher . . . heav-
ier. . . . " In this seesawing of the scale of odors, I
was lost, I could no longer discern the direction of the
memory I should follow: I knew only that at one point
of the spectrum, there was a gap, a secret fold where
there lurked that perfume which, for me, was a complete woman.

And wasn't it, after all, the same thing in the savan-
nah, the forest, the swamp, when they were a network
of smells, and we ran along, heads down, never losing
contact with the ground, using hands and noses to help
us find the trail? We understood whatever there was to
understand through our noses rather than through our
eyes: the mammoth, the porcupine, onion, drought, rain
are first smells which become distinct from other smells;
food, non-food; our cave, the enemy's cave; danger—
everything is first perceived by the nose, everything is
within the nose, the world is the nose. In our herd, our

nose tells us who belongs to the herd and who doesn't;
the herd's females have a smell that is the herd's smell,
but each female also has an odor that distinguishes her
from the other females. Between us and them, at first
sight, there isn't much difference: we're all made the
same way, and besides, what's the point of standing
there staring? Odor, that's what each of us has that's
different from the others. The odor tells you immediately and certainly what you need to know. There are
no words, there is no information more precise than
what the nose receives. With my nose I learned that in
the herd there is a female not like the others, not like
the others for me, for my nose; and I ran, following
her trail in the grass, my nose exploring all the females
running in front of me, of my nose, in the herd; and
there I found her, it was she who had summoned me
with her odor in the midst of all those odors; there, I
breathed through my nose all of her and her love-
summons. The herd moves, keeps running, trotting, and
if you stop, in the herd's stampede, they are all on top
of you, trampling you, confusing your nose with their
smells; and now I'm on top of her, and they are push-
ing us, overturning us; they all climb on her, on me;
all the females sniff me; all the males and females become tangled with us, and all their smells, which have
nothing to do with that smell I smelled before and now
smell no longer. It is waiting for me to hunt for it. I
hunt for her spoor in the dusty, trampled grass. I sniff.
I sniff all the females. I no longer recognize her. I force
my way desperately through the herd, hunting for her
with my nose.

FOR that matter, now that I wake up in the smell of grass and turn my hand to make a *zlwan zlwan zlwan* with the brush on the drum, echoing Patrick's *tlann tlann* on his four strings, because I think I'm still playing She knows and I know, but actually there was just Lenny knocking himself out, sweating like a horse, with his twelve strings, and one of those birds from Hampstead kneeling there and doing some things to him, while I was playing *ding bong dang yang*, and all the others including me were off. I was lying flat, the drums had fallen and I hadn't even noticed, I reach out to pull the drums to safety or else they'll kick them in, those round things I see, white in the darkness, I reach out and I touch flesh, by its smell it seems warm girl's flesh, I hunt for the drums which have rolled on the floor in the darkness with the beer cans, with all the others who have rolled on the floor naked, in the upset ashtrays, a nice warm ass in the air, and saying it's not so hot you can sleep naked on the floor, of course there are a lot of us shut up in here for God knows how long, but somebody has to put more shillings in the gas stove that's gone out and is making nothing but a stink, and, out as I was, I woke up in a cold sweat all the fault of the lousy shit they gave us to smoke, the ones who brought us to this stinking place down by the docks with the excuse that here we could make all the racket we liked all night long without having the fuzz on our tails like always, and we had to go someplace anyway after they threw us out of that dump in Portobello Road, but it was because they wanted to make these new birds

that came after us from Hampstead and we didn't even
have time to see who they were or what they looked
like, because we always have a whole swarm of groupies
after us when we play somewhere, and specially when
Robin breaks into Have mercy, have mercy on me, those
birds turn on and want to do things right away, and so
all the others begin while we're still up there sweating
and playing and I'm hitting those drums *ba-zoom ba-*
zoom ba-zoom, and they're at it, Have mercy on me,
have mercy on me, ma'am, and so tonight, just like the
other times, we didn't do anything with these groupies
even if they do follow our bunch so logically we ought
to make it with them, not those others.

So now I get up to hunt for this lousy gas stove to
put some shillings in it and make it go, I walk with the
soles of my feet on hair asses butts beer cans tits glasses
of whisky spilled on the carpet, somebody must have
thrown up on it too, I better go on all fours, at least I
can see where I'm going, and besides I can't stand up
straight, so I recognize people by the smell, our bunch
with all that sweat sticking to us is easy to recognize, I
can tell us from the others who stink only of their lousy
grass and their dirty hair, and the girls too who don't
take many baths, but their smells mix with the others a
little and are a little different from the others as well,
and every now and then you run into some special smells
on these girls and it's worth lingering a minute and
sniffing, their hair for example, when it doesn't absorb
too much smoke, and in other places too, logically, and
so I am crossing the room, smelling some of these smells
of sleeping girls until at one point I stop.

As I say, it's hard really to smell one girl's skin, especially when you're all in a big tangle of bodies, but there beneath me I'm surely smelling a girl's white skin, a white smell with that special force white has, a slightly mottled skin smell probably dotted with faint or even invisible freckles, a skin that breathes the way a leaf's pores breathe the meadows, and all the stink in the room keeps its distance from this skin, maybe two inches, maybe two fractions of an inch, because meanwhile I start inhaling this skin everywhere while she sleeps with her face hidden in her arms, her long maybe red hair over her shoulders down her back, her long legs outstretched, cool in the pockets behind the knees, now I really am breathing and smelling nothing but her, who must have felt, still sleeping, that I am smelling her and must not mind, because she rises on her elbows, her face still held down, and from her armpit I move and smell what her breast is like, the tip, and since I'm kind of astride, logically it seems the right moment to push in the direction that makes me happy and I feel she's happy too, so, half-sleeping, we find a way of lying and agree on how I should lie and how she should now beautifully lie.

Meanwhile the cold we haven't been feeling we feel afterwards and I remember I was on my way to put shillings in the stove, and I get up, I break away from the island of her smell, I go on crossing among unknown bodies, among smells that are incompatible, or rather repulsive, I hunt in the others' things to see if I can find some shillings, following the gas-stink I hunt for the stove and I make it work, gasping and stinking more than ever, following its loo stink I hunt for the loo and I piss there, shivering in the gray light of morning that trickles from the little window, I go back into the darkness, the stagnation, the exhalation of the bodies, now I have to cross them again to find that girl I know only by her smell, it's hard to hunt in the dark but even if I saw her how can I tell it's her when all I know is her smell, so I go on smelling the bodies lying on the floor and one guy says fuck off and punches me, this place is laid out in a funny way, like a lot of rooms with people lying on the floor in all of them, and I've lost my sense of direction or else I never had one, these girls have different smells, some might even be her only the smell isn't the same any more, meanwhile Howard's waked up and he's already got his bass and he's picking up Don't tell me I'm through, I think I've already covered the whole place, so where has she gone, in the midst of these girls you can begin to see now the light's coming in, but what I want to smell I can't smell, I'm roaming around like a jerk and I can't find her, Have mercy, have mercy on me, I go from one skin to another hunting for that lost skin that isn't like any other skin.

FOR each woman a perfume exists which enhances the perfume of her own skin, the note in the scale which is at once color and flavor and aroma and tenderness, and thus the pleasure in moving from one skin to another can be endless. When the chandeliers in the Faubourg Saint-Honoré's drawing rooms illuminated my entrance

into the gala balls, I was overwhelmed by the pungent
cloud of perfumes from the pearl-edged decolletés, the
delicate Bulgarian-pink ground giving off jabs of cam-
phor which amber made cling to the silk dresses, and I
bowed to kiss the Duchesse du Havre-Caumartin's hand,
inhaling the jasmine that hovered over her slightly ane-
mic skin, and I offered my arm to the Comtesse de
Barbès-Rochechouart, who ensnared me in the wave of
sandalwood that seemed to engulf her firm, dark com-
plexion, and I helped the Baronne de Mouton-Duver-
net free her alabaster shoulder from her otter coat as a
gust of fuchsia struck me. My papillae could easily as-
sign faces to those perfumes Madame Odile now had
me review, removing the stoppers from her opalescent
vials. I had devoted myself to the same process the night
before at the masked ball of the Knights of the Holy
Sepulchre; there was no lady whose name I could not
guess beneath the embroidered domino. But then she
appeared, with a little satin mask over her face, a veil
around her shoulders and bosom, Andalusian style; and
in vain I wondered who she was, and in vain, holding
her closer than was proper as we danced, I compared
my memories with that perfume never imagined until
then, which enclosed the perfume of her body as an
oyster encloses its pearl. I knew nothing of her, but I
felt I knew all in that perfume; and I would have desired a world without names, where that perfume alone
would have sufficed as name and as all the words she
could speak to me: that perfume I knew was lost now
in Madame Odile's liquid labyrinth, evaporated in my

memory, so that I could not summon it back even by remembering her when she followed me into the conservatory with the hydrangeas. As I caressed her, she seemed at times docile, then at times violent, clawing. She allowed me to uncover hidden areas, explore the privacy of her perfume, provided I did not raise the mask from her face.

"Why this mystery, after all?" I cried, exasperated. "Tell me where and when I can see you once more. Or rather, see you for the first time!"

"Do not think of such a thing, Monsieur," she answered. "A terrible threat hangs over my life. But hush— there he is!"

A shadow, hooded, in a violet domino, had appeared in the Empire mirror.

"I must follow that person," the woman said. "Forget me. Someone holds unspeakable power over me."

And before I could say to her, "My sword is at your service. Have faith in it!", she had already gone off, preceding the violet domino, which left a wake of Oriental tobacco in the crowd of maskers. I do not know through which door they succeeded in slipping away. I followed them in vain, and in vain I plagued with questions all those familiar with le tout Paris. I know I shall have no peace until I have found the trail of that hostile odor and that beloved perfume, until one has put me on the trail of the other, until the duel in which I shall kill my enemy has given me the right to tear away the mask concealing that face.

THERE is a hostile odor that strikes my nose every time
I think I've caught the odor of the female I am hunting
for in the trail of the herd, a hostile odor also mixed
with her odor, and I bare my incisors, canines, pre-
molars, and I am already filled with rage, I gather stones,
I tear off knotty branches, if I cannot find with my
nose that smell of hers I would like to have at least the
satisfaction of finding out the owner of this hostile odor
that makes me angry. The herd has sudden shifts of
direction when the whole stream turns on you, and
suddenly I feel my jaws slammed to the ground by a
club's blow on my skull, a kick jabs into my neck, and
with my nose I recognize the hostile male who has recognized on me his female's odor, and he tries to finish
me off by flinging me against the rock, and I recognize
her smell on him and I am filled with fury, I jump up,
I swing my club with all my strength until I smell the
odor of blood, I leap on him with my full weight, I
batter his skull with flints, shards, elkjaws, bones, dag-
gers, horn harpoons, while all the females form a circle
around us, waiting to see who will win. Obviously, I
win, I stand up and grope among the females, but I
cannot find the one I am looking for; caked with blood
and dust, I cannot smell odors very clearly any more,
so I might as well stand on my hind legs and walk erect
for a while.

Some of us have got into the habit of walking like
this, never putting hands on the ground, and some can
even move fast. It makes my head swim a little, and I

raise my hands to cling to boughs as I used to when I
lived in trees all the time, but now I notice that I can
keep my balance even up there, my foot flattens against
the ground, and my legs move forward even if I don't
bend my knees. Of course, by keeping my nose suspended up here in the air, I lose a lot of things: information you get by sniffing the earth with all the spoors
of animals that move over it, sniffing the others in the
herd, specially the females. But you get other things
instead: your nose is drier, so you can pick up distant
smells carried by the wind, and you find fruit on the
trees, birds' eggs in their nests. And your eyes help
your nose, they grasp things in space—the sycamore's
leaves, the river, the blue stripe of the forest, the clouds.

IN the end, I go out to breathe in the morning, the
street, the fog, all you can see in dustbins: fish scales,
cans, nylon stockings; at the corner a Pakistani who
sells pineapples has opened his shop; I reach a wall of
fog and it's the Thames. From the railing, if you look
hard, you can see the shadows of the same old tugs,
you can smell the same mud and oil, and farther on the
lights and smoke of Southwark begin. And I bang my
head against the fog like I was accompanying that gui-
tar chord of In the morning I'll be dead, and I can't get
it out of my mind.

WITH a splitting headache, I leave the *parfumerie*; I
would like to rush immediately to the Passy address I
wrested from Madame Odile after many obscure hints

and conjectures, but instead I shout to my driver: "The Bois, Auguste! At once! A brisk trot!"

And as soon as the phaeton moves, I breathe deeply to free myself of all the scents that have mingled in my brain, I savor the leather smell of the upholstery and the trappings, the stink of the horse and his steaming dung and urine, I smell again the thousand odors, stately or plebeian, which fly in the air of Paris, and it is only when the sycamores of the Bois de Boulogne have plunged me into the lymph of their foliage, when the gardeners' water stirs an earthy smell from the clover, that I order Auguste to turn toward Passy.

The door of the house is half-open. There are people going in, men in top hats, veiled ladies. Already in the hall I am struck by a heavy smell of flowers, as of rotting vegetation; I enter, among the glowing beeswax tapers, the chrysanthemum wreaths, the cushions of violets, the asphodel garlands. In the open, satin-lined coffin, the face is unrecognizable, covered by a veil and swathed in bandages, as if in the decomposition of her features her beauty continues to reject death; but I recognize the base, the echo of that perfume that resembles no other, merged with the odor of death now as if they had always been inseparable.

I would like to question someone, but all these people are strangers, perhaps foreigners. I pause beside an elderly man who looks the most foreign of all: an olive-skinned gentleman with a red fez and a black frock coat, standing in meditation beside the bier. "To think that

at midnight she was dancing, and was the loveliest
woman at the ball. . . . "

The man with the fez does not turn, but answers in
a low voice: "What do you mean, sir? At midnight she
was dead."

STANDING erect, with my nose in the wind, I perceive
less precise signs, but of vaster meaning, signs that bring
with them suspicion, alarm, horror, signs that when you
have your nose to the ground you refuse perhaps to
accept, you turn away from them, as I turn from this
odor which comes from the rocks of the chasm where
we in our herd fling animals we've disemboweled, the
rotting organs, the bones, where the vultures hover and
circle. And that odor I was following was lost down
there, and, depending on how the wind blows, it rises
with the stink of the clawed cadavers, the breath of the
jackals that tear them apart still warm in the blood that
is drying on the rocks in the sun.

AND when I go back upstairs to hunt for the others
because my head feels a little clearer and maybe now I
could find her again and figure out who she is, instead
there was nobody up there, God knows when they went
away, while I was down on the Embankment, all the
rooms are empty except for the beer cans and my drums,
and the stove's stink has become unbearable, and I move
around all the rooms and there is one with the door
locked, the very room with the stove you can smell
gasping through the cracks in the door, so strong it's

nauseating, and I begin to slam my shoulder against the door until it gives way, and inside the place is all full of thick, black, disgusting gás from floor to ceiling, and on the floor the thing I see before I writhe in a fit of vomiting is the long, white, outstretched form, face hidden by the hair, and as I pull her out by her stiffened legs I smell her odor within the asphyxiating odor, her odor that I try to follow and distinguish in the ambulance, in the first-aid room, among the odors of disinfectant and slime that drips from the marble slabs in the morgue, and the air is impregnated with it, especially when outside the weather is damp.

January, 1972
Paris

NOTE

IN 1972 Calvino started writing a book about the five senses. At his death, in 1985, only three stories had been completed: "Under the Jaguar Sun," "A King Listens," and "The Name, the Nose." Had he lived, this book would certainly have evolved into something quite different.

In the light of Calvino's previous works and given what he said to me—"How shall I make a book out of this?"—I believe he would not have stopped with sight and touch, the two "missing" senses. He would have provided a frame, as in *If on a winter's night a traveler,* a frame that amounts to another novel, virtually a book in itself.

In fact, in notes written a few days before he fell ill—when he had started to think about the book's overall structure—Calvino refers to the importance of the frame and defines it:

Both in art and in literature, the function of the frame is fundamental. It is the frame that marks the boundary between the picture and what is outside. It allows the picture to exist, isolating it from the rest; but at the same time, it recalls—and somehow stands for—everything that remains out of the picture. I might venture a definition: we consider poetic a production in which each individual experience acquires prominence through its detachment from the general continuum, while it retains a kind of glint of that unlimited vastness.

In any case, I would prefer the reader to consider *Under the Jaguar Sun* not as something Calvino started and left unfinished but simply as three stories written in different periods of his life.

Esther Calvino